FASHION
ACADEMY

Fashion
Face-Off

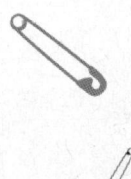

Also by Sheryl Berk and Carrie Berk

The Cupcake Club Series

The Cupcake Club

Recipe for Trouble

Winner Bakes All

Icing on the Cake

Baby Cakes

Royal Icing

Sugar and Spice

Sweet Victory

Bakers on Board

Vote for Cupcakes!

Hugs and Sprinkles

Fashion Academy Series

Fashion Academy

Runway Ready

Designer Drama

Model Madness

FASHION
ACADEMY

Fashion Face-Off

Sheryl Berk & Carrie Berk

sourcebooks
jabberwocky

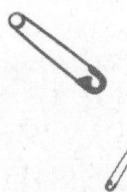

Published by Sourcebooks Jabberwocky, an imprint of Sourcebooks, Inc.
P.O. Box 4410, Naperville, Illinois 60567-4410
(630) 961-3900
Fax: (630) 961-2168
www.sourcebooks.com

Library of Congress Cataloging-in-Publication data is on file with the publisher.

Source of Production: Versa Press, East Peoria, Illinois, USA
Date of Production: May 2017
Run Number: 5009461

Printed and bound in the United States of America.
VP 10 9 8 7 6 5 4 3 2 1

To Stacie, Lauren, and all the ECUSA and East Coast

Starz kids who rock the runway and dream BIG!

Seen On-Screen

"Pass the popcorn, will ya?" JC refused to look away from the TV—not even for a split second.

Mickey Williams sighed. Sometimes her fashion school bestie could be such a diva! Yet over the past two semesters, since she left Philadelphia to attend the Fashion Academy of Brooklyn (a.k.a. FAB), she'd gotten used to his quirky behavior. FAB now felt like home, and so did her aunt Olive's brownstone on the Upper West Side of

Manhattan—although Mickey missed her mom and counted the days till she could take the train back to see her.

On that first fateful day, JC had shown Mickey around the school, sat with her at lunch, and filled her in on all the ins and outs of what made FAB the top training ground for future fashion designers. He warned her about which teachers (Mr. Kaye) were super tough and which students (Jade Lee) were trouble. Jade tried her best to belittle Mickey's style and talent, but JC was always there to back her up with a snappy one-liner: "Gee, Jade, jealous much? Green is so not your color…"

If Mickey was feeling frustrated or confused

by a homework assignment, JC knew just how to cheer her up, usually with a pep talk and an eighties pop tune. And whenever she was in a pinch—fashion-wise or otherwise—he came to her rescue.

She looked at JC and shrugged. He could be annoying, but he was an awesome friend. "Okay, here's your popcorn," she said, waving it under his nose.

"Oh, and Madonna needs one of her treats." He motioned toward his Chihuahua's dog carrier in the corner of Mickey's living room. "Would ya mind?"

"Really?" Mickey groaned. "Do I look like a waitress?"

JC glanced at her quickly. "Actually, you look more like an eggplant today." He pointed to the purple hair chalk she'd used to highlight her hair. "I'm digging the violet velvet bomber jacket though. Nice tailoring."

Mickey smiled. She'd gotten up at 5:00 a.m. to put the finishing touches on her latest design. Of course, JC had noticed it.

He also noticed that one of the contestants on the show had suddenly burst into tears. "No, Nigel!" he yelled at the sobbing designer. "You can do it! Don't crack under the pressure, dude!"

Mickey laughed. While she loved *Assignment: Fashion*, she was nowhere near as obsessed with the show as JC. For him, the finale was like the Super Bowl of style.

"He's got to man up!" JC shouted at the TV. "Don't fumble this, Nigel! This is a make-or-break fashion moment!"

JC sat back down and shoveled more popcorn in his mouth. "Oh, and lemonade... I could use a refill." He handed Mickey his glass, still staring at the screen.

"So let me get this straight," Mickey said, observing the four semifinalists frantically attempting to make an outfit out of tinfoil and paper streamers. "They can't use fabric at all...not even muslin for the foundation?"

"It's the 'out-of-left-field challenge,'" JC explained. "You have to work with whatever they toss you—in this case party paper goods. The materials are never anything you'd think of using for an outfit."

"Speak for yourself," Mickey said. "I'd be great at this. I once made a T-shirt out of cabbage leaves."

"I recall." JC fanned the air with his hand. "My nose will never forget it." He leaned forward, practically crawling inside the TV screen. "Did you see that? Did you see how Ignacio did that whipstitch on his cardboard moto jacket? With Helga Floom barking at him to get his model and his butt out to the runway?"

"I saw, I saw," Mickey said, offering Madonna a tiny bone-shaped biscuit. "And speaking of barking..."

She noticed that Madonna had curled up on the wool throw on the couch—and was getting crumbs all over it. "My aunt Olive is going to be home soon, and she won't appreciate a dog being here."

"A dog? Madonna is not a dog. She's a fashion icon," JC said, defending his pup. He scooped her in his arms. "This black satin dress took me hours to make. Did you notice the pearl detail around the neckline?"

"Very impressive," Mickey replied. JC was an

absolute genius when it came to designing dog-wear. "But Olive's more of a bird person…"

Just then, Mickey heard a key turning in the lock. Olive walked into the foyer, flustered as usual.

"You wouldn't believe the day I had, Mackenzie," she called to her niece. "I had to stay overtime just to get those legal briefs in decent shape." Mickey knew that her aunt took her job as a legal secretary very seriously.

"I invited JC over," Mickey warned her. "And Madonna."

"Who's Madonna?" Olive asked. Then her nostrils zoned in on something. "Is that liver I smell?" She walked in to find Mickey, JC, and a tiny dog in a dress sprawled on her couch.

JC examined the treat box. "Yup, liver and bacon...Madonna's fave flavors."

Olive cringed. "I'm a vegan," she said. "The smell makes me queasy."

Mickey quickly grabbed the box and tossed it into JC's bag. "Right, which is why we are putting them away." She elbowed JC in the ribs. "And apologizing."

"Ow! Sorry. Madonna's a liver lover. She can't help herself."

Olive rubbed her temples. "I'm exhausted. I'm

going to sleep early. Mackenzie, please make sure you tidy up after your friend leaves."

Mickey nodded. "Absolutely. 'Night, Aunt Olive."

When Olive had closed the bedroom door behind her, JC put his feet up on the coffee table. "I think the top three will be Ignacio, Illiana, and Bootsie," he said, sounding like a sports announcer. "Ignacio's got skills…and a cool head. Iliana is a wizard with mixing patterns. But Nigel can't take the pressure. He's falling apart at the seams. I think it's gonna be Bootsie for the win. She's got a classy aesthetic. Very forties glam."

"No way," Mickey insisted. "It's gotta be

Ignacio. I have never seen anyone so creative. He's always thinking out of the box."

"Classic will trump fashion forward. Wait and see," JC asserted. "The judges always go with what's the most marketable collection."

"And you don't think out of the box has a market?" Mickey asked, slightly peeved. Was he *actually* dissing her design style?

"I do, but in general, I think more shoppers are nostalgic for the old days," JC insisted. "Marilyn Monroe, Grace Kelly, Jackie O… Who wouldn't want to dress like those women?" He held up his dog. "Madonna certainly does. This dress was inspired by Audrey Hepburn."

Mickey groaned. "She's a dog. She's not going shopping in a department store."

"Shh!" JC hushed her. "She's very sensitive about the *d-o-g* word, so let's not use it."

"Oh, for goodness' sake!" Mickey said, pulling a couch pillow over her head. "JC, you're ridiculous."

"Talented…stylish…genius perhaps. Ridiculous? Never."

Just then, the commercial ended, and the judges on *Assignment: Fashion* took their seats.

"That was quite an amazing runway!" the host, supermodel Helga Floom, enthused. "This was a very difficult decision, but we have our top three finalists."

JC grabbed Mickey's hand. "I can't stand the suspense! Spill it, Helga!"

"Nigel, I'm sorry," the host began. "Your assignment here is over."

JC jumped up and down on the couch. "Yes! Yes! Yes! I called it!"

Mickey clicked Off on the remote. "And we'll have to tune in next week to see who wins— Illiana, Bootsie, or Ignacio."

"Bootsie has it in the bag," JC said, tucking Madonna into her dog carrier and slinging it over his shoulder.

"And I say it's Ignacio," Mickey teased him. "Care to make a small wager?"

"Whaddya have in mind?" JC replied, raising an eyebrow.

"The loser has to make the winner a fabulous outfit—to his or her specifications."

JC held out his hand to shake on it. "Done. I'm going to want a varsity jacket for Madonna in violet velvet," he said. "With a big *M* on the back."

Mickey ushered him out the door. "And I want a black satin skirt," she said. "You can hold the pearl trim and maybe give me something a little more original."

JC snickered. "I've watched thirteen seasons and never *not* picked the winner."

Mickey smiled back. "Well, there's a first time for everything!"

2

★ Let the Games Begin! ★

A week later, Mickey was working on her assigned reading for her History of Fabrics class when JC called to brag.

"Told ya so! Bootise takes the win."

"What?" Mickey asked. "Did I miss it?" She had completely forgotten the new episode of *Assignment: Fashion* was on tonight.

"Uh, yeah. It's been on for the past hour. What have you been doing?"

"Reading about how flax fibers are spun to

make linen." She sighed. Mickey picked up her textbook and recited aloud: "You pick the plants and then soak them in a tub of water until the hard outside stem rots away and leaves the long, soft fibers behind…"

"Ooh, fascinating," JC teased. "I'm on the edge of my seat."

"Tell me about it," Mickey said, flipping through the chapter. "I have twenty more pages left. We're having a quiz tomorrow, and I have to know everything from linen to pashmina."

"Well, when you're done, you can start designing Madonna's varsity jacket. Time to pay up. A bet is a bet."

"Fine," Mickey said. "It sounds a lot more fun than my homework!"

The next morning, Mickey was so tired from studying, she was almost late to her first period Advanced Apparel Arts class.

She stifled a yawn as Jade Lee strolled in and sat down at her drawing table in the first row. She was dressed to the nines as usual in a pink satin bomber jacket, a white sweater dress, and a rhinestone tiara-like headband. Mickey noticed that her shoes sparkled as well. Jade had on the latest Saint Laurent metallic booties in a silver camo print.

Her twin brother, Jake, trailed behind her, also dressed in the finest couture: a Comme des Garçons sweater that Mickey had seen in *Vogue* for three hundred and fifty dollars. She reminded herself that the twins' mother, designer-to-the-stars Bridget Lee, gave them everything. Mickey looked down at her own boots: a pair of old, scuffed Dr. Martens she'd speckled with neon-yellow paint. She curled her feet behind her under the chair. Jade would get a good laugh out of them.

Just then, Jade spun around in her seat. "You," she said, addressing Mickey.

Mickey looked around. "Me?"

"Yes, *you*. Did you hear anything about Kaye's final?"

Mickey shrugged. "No. I mean, why would he tell me?"

Jade rolled her eyes. "Because you're always trying to get in his good graces with your hideous fashion fiascos."

"Her designs aren't bad. They're original," her classmate Mars piped up. She, of all people, understood what it was to be avant-garde. Her jewelry was made out of everything from safety pins to bottle caps. "Mickey's got a really great eye."

"Yeah," chimed in South, another classmate. "I like your fringe vest. It's very Coachella." South's dad was a famous rap star, so she was always hanging out in the VIP section at concerts and festivals. "I think I saw Kendall Jenner wearing one like it. Then again, she was a few rows behind me…"

Jade smirked. "Pullease. I doubt Mickey even looked in the mirror this morning." She pointed to Mickey's yellow-plaid skirt, black suede vest, and purple-striped sweater. Mickey had found all the pieces in a thrift store back home in Philly and reworked them.

Jade took out a pocket mirror from her purse

and held it open to Mickey. "See? You look like a color-blind bumblebee."

Gabriel was seated next to Mickey and laughed out loud. "Sorry, Mickey," he apologized. "But you gotta admit, that was pretty funny."

Mickey shook her head and sighed. She knew better than to get into an argument with Jade. It never ended well. Instead, she buried her head in her sketchbook and remembered what her mom always said about bullies: "Don't engage. Ignore them."

Gabriel changed the topic back to Mr. Kaye's final. "The man is merciless. I failed last year, which is why I had to take this class over."

"What was it like?" Mars asked.

"It was sick," Gabriel said.

Jake gasped. "That hard?"

"No *sick*…as in ill," Gabriel explained. "We had to use hospital gowns and surgical scrubs for the materials. Personally, I thought my use of the stethoscope for a necktie was a nice touch, but Kaye called it 'too literal.' Then he gave me an F."

"I've heard that Kaye's finals are the hardest in the entire school," South said.

Mickey gulped. Up till this point, she'd been feeling pretty confident that she would earn straight A's her first year at FAB. But now she wasn't so sure. She glanced at the clock on the wall: it read 8:59 a.m. Their teacher was never late—which meant he would be bursting in the door in five…four…three…two…

"Get your sketchbooks out!" boomed a voice. The students jumped to attention as Mr. Kaye swept in, threw his jacket and briefcase on his desk, and began to dictate.

"Congratulations, you've all made it to the final assignment of the semester," he said. "Think of this as the World Series of Advanced Apparel Arts. The question is, who will strike out and who will knock it out of the park?"

"Oh no." Gabriel sank in his seat. "Here it comes. When he gets punny, it's never a good thing."

"Each of you will be given uniforms and gear to use for your material."

Jade's hand shot up. "A uniform? You mean like what my chauffeur wears every day? Ewww…"

"No, I mean a team uniform—baseball, basketball, football, hockey." He pointed to a large cardboard box in the corner and walked over to it. "I think you'll find this a nice sampling." He pulled out a New York Knicks jersey in royal blue and orange. "You may supplement your provided material with additional fabric and trim costing no more than thirty dollars."

This time, Jake raised his hand. "So you want us to redesign a team uniform?"

"I want you to turn it upside down, inside out, and on its head," Kaye insisted. "I want to see imagination in repurposing these clothes."

"So we should use them to make something totally *not* sporty," Mickey asked. "Like a tuxedo out of a tracksuit."

Jade chuckled. "A tuxedo? Out of a sweaty shirt that says 'New York 23' on it? Yeah, good luck with that."

"If you can do that, I see a home run in your future, Mackenzie," Mr. Kaye said.

"This is worse than the sick challenge," Gabriel moaned. "I'm doomed."

"You will have two weeks to complete your

look. And do not, I repeat, do not disappoint me."

He stepped back from the box, referee whistle in hand. "On your mark, get set…go!" He blew the whistle, and everyone ran for the container, pushing and shoving and clawing at the clothes inside it. Jade, of course, got there first and managed to elbow everyone else out of her way while she color-coordinated her materials.

Mickey reached over Mars's head and pulled out a few pieces without even seeing them. "Is this a vest?" she asked, examining a shapeless, green mesh tank.

"I think it's called a pinnie," Gabriel said. He

handed her one of his castoffs—a yellow soccer shirt. "Make sure you get lots to work with. You can always scrap one if you don't like it. But you don't want to come up short."

Mickey nodded and squeezed her arm in between South and Jake who were playing tug-of-war with a pair of red sweatpants. She pulled out several more pieces and threw them over her shoulders. One was a hoodie; another a pin-striped baseball jersey. When she finally got to peer inside the box, there were only baseball hats and a few referee whistles remaining. She scooped up a bunch of caps and crossed her fingers that she'd gotten enough. She hoped that something, anything, would ignite her creativity. Her grade depended on it!

The Perfect Mix

At home that night, Mickey spilled out all the materials she'd managed to snag: a Rangers hockey jersey, a pair of yellow-and-purple Lakers shorts, several pairs of sweatpants, and a black ribbed running tank. She placed a baseball cap on her head and tried to think. The problem was that none of the pieces seemed to go together. Had she actually suggested making a tuxedo? Out of *this*?

Aunt Olive poked her head into Mickey's bedroom. "Care for a slice of my Very Veggie Casserole? It's filled with leeks, zucchini, eggplant, peppers, broccoli, carrots, and squash—with vegan grated cheese on top."

Mickey wrinkled her nose. "Um, thanks, Aunt Olive, but I'm not that hungry."

Her aunt waved a plate. "You sure? Hot out of the oven! I'll just leave it here in case you change your mind." She placed the dish on the nightstand next to Mickey's bed. The slice was an odd layered mixture of green, orange, and purple in a crust spotted with yellowy flakes that Mickey assumed were the shreds of vegan cheese.

Olive noticed her hesitation. "I know it doesn't look pretty, but it tastes delicious," she insisted. "Try just a forkful. I promise, you'll love it."

Mickey took a tiny piece and placed it on the tip of her tongue. Hmm…it wasn't bad. She took another bite, and another, and another.

"Told ya so!" Olive beamed. "All the flavors of the veggies just meld together…and the texture too."

She was absolutely right, Mickey thought. This strange combination *did* create culinary magic. "Can I have seconds?" she asked her aunt.

"Comin' right up!" Olive replied, racing back to the kitchen.

Mickey stared down at the pile of uniforms and accessories. Like her aunt's ingredients, they were all different colors and textures. She picked up a yellow tee and placed it on top of an orange hoodie—then laid a green baseball hat on top. Maybe that was her problem. Next to each other, they didn't work, but if she chopped up the pieces and mixed them into layers…

She grabbed a pair of scissors and started cutting.

"My goodness!" Olive exclaimed, reappearing with a second helping of casserole. "Why are you killing those clothes?"

"I'm creating a recipe," Mickey explained,

using her colored pencils to sketch how the scraps would come together. "A pinch of this, a sprinkle of that," she muttered to herself. She was completely in *the zone* as she liked to call it—the moment when her design sprang to life from her imagination onto the page of her sketchbook.

And with any luck, the result would be as yummy as Olive's dinner—or at least enough to whet Mr. Kaye's appetite.

"I'm speechless," Mr. Kaye said, shaking his head.

Mickey didn't know if that was good or bad—or

if showing him her drawing the next morning was the best idea. But she needed the feedback.

"I know it's a little out there," she tried to explain.

"It is…but in a jaw-droppingly brilliant way. What you're attempting…well, it's very exciting. I've never seen anything like it."

Jaw-dropping. Brilliant. Exciting. Mickey could hardly believe her ears. Did he mean *her* sketch?

"Carry on, Mackenzie," he added. "This design has a great deal of potential."

Mickey floated out of his office—and nearly crashed head-on into Jade, who was strolling down the hall taking selfies of her OOTD.

"Watch it, weirdo," Jade snapped. "You almost got in my Instagram shot."

"Sorry!" Mickey replied. "I was just coming from Mr. Kaye's office…"

"Of course you were." Jade snickered. "Were you begging for help—or an extension?"

"Neither," Mickey said, clutching her sketchbook tightly to her chest. "I have an idea, and he likes it…a lot. He said it was jaw-droppingly brilliant."

Jade's face grew pale. "Well, I'm sure it's not nearly as good as my design."

"I wouldn't be too sure of that," Mickey taunted her. "But you'll just have to wait to see."

She snapped her fingers in the air and walked

away. JC was waiting by her locker. "You should have been there," she told him. "I think I actually just scared the sequins off Jade."

"How'd ya do that? Take away her platinum AMEX card?" JC joked.

"I told her how much Mr. Kaye loved my final project design."

JC looked worried. "Careful, Mick. Kaye has a really short memory. He could totally change his mind tomorrow. Like Helga says on *Assignment: Fashion*, 'One day you're hot. The next day you're not.'"

"Don't be silly," Mickey insisted. "He called it brilliant and exciting. And I'm gonna score a goal or a home run—or whatever you do to win in football."

JC chuckled. "You mean a touchdown. And I hope so." He pointed to Jade who had Jake by the arm and was whispering in his ear. "'Cause Jade is *not* a good sport."

Copycat

The two weeks flew by, and Mickey was putting the finishing touches on her final project. She had shown it to no one—not JC, not Aunt Olive, not even her mom whom she always FaceTimed when she was working on her assignments.

"Can't I get a little sneak peek?" her mom had pleaded.

Mickey shook her head. "Nope, not till I present it in class. It's top secret, but I will tell you I'm really proud of it."

"And I'm proud of you," her mom replied. "You've had an amazing first year at FAB. You've worked hard, and you've proven yourself a talented designer. Which I always knew you were…"

"We'll see what Mr. Kaye says," Mickey said, twirling a strand of hair around her finger. "JC says he's fashion fickle."

Her mom chuckled. "Meaning what?"

"Meaning he could say he likes my sketch and then hate my final design."

"That won't happen," her mom promised her. "I believe in you, Mick. You get your brains from me, after all."

"And my style!" Mickey piped up. Her mom

was the one who had taught her to shop at flea markets and fearlessly combine old and new, leather and lace, plaid and polka dot. She was a makeup artist who brought artistry into everything she did, from her outfits to her homemade breakfasts.

"So I'll be home this weekend. Can we have pineapple chocolate-chip pancakes with whipped cream and rainbow sprinkles?" Mickey asked.

"I already went shopping for the ingredients," her mom said. "I'm one step ahead of you."

But before she could go home to Philly for her mom's special Sunday breakfast, there was the not-so-small matter of her Advance Apparel Arts final presentation. Mickey carefully packed her design in its garment bag and carried it delicately over her arm as she climbed onto the school bus.

As she sat there, watching the traffic on the Brooklyn Bridge whiz by outside the window, she tried to think back to the first day she had taken this ride. Then, she was a nervous newbie who pictured herself taking FAB by storm. In reality, it had been a much harder road. She'd had to prove herself time and time again and learn to trust her instincts. Mr. Kaye always told her that the best designers are true to themselves—and that's what she'd always been. Even if her classmates— especially Jade—thought she was weird and her designs were bizarre, everything Mickey created came from her heart.

As the bus pulled up to FAB, she stepped off and climbed the steps to the school entrance. This was the exact spot where she had first met JC. He had spotted her coming off the bus and made a beeline for the clueless new girl who needed help. She was no longer that girl. Now she had confidence and could easily find her way around the halls and studios. She held her head high at FAB; she was one of them.

"Big day!" said a voice sneaking up behind her. Mickey jumped.

"JC! You scared me!"

"You're scared? I'm giving my final presentation today in my Sequins and Studs class. Ms. Rollings said she's deducting one full letter grade for every dropped stitch. I was up all night with a magnifying glass making sure I had none."

"Did you do the Dalmatian-print jumpsuit you told me about?"

JC winked. "With white-and-black sequin spots. It's beyond."

"She'll love it," Mickey assured him. It was a very clever play on the project theme, "Get to the point," as well as a perfect way to showcase JC's love for all things canine.

"I made Madonna a mini version," he said,

unzipping his bag. Madonna's tiny head popped up. She was wearing a sequin-dotted dress and a pearl collar.

Mickey giggled. "Beyond!"

Then she checked the time on her phone. First period would be starting in fifteen minutes. "Wish me luck," she told her friend and squeezed his hand.

"Break a heel," he said. "That's fashion-speak for go slay it!"

When she got to the studio, she was shocked

that Jade wasn't already there unwrapping her work. Usually she was the first one in, eager to show off.

Mickey rolled her dress form next to her desk, unzipped the garment bag, and gently lifted the fabric out. She began dressing the figure in the huge, ruffled ball gown. Each of the layers of the skirt was made from assorted uniforms. The colors formed a billowy rainbow, and the skirt itself reminded Mickey of a ball.

South walked in, and her jaw dropped.

"Mickey, that's…that's…" she stammered.

"I know. I worked so hard on it. I think it's really original."

"No, it's not," South told her. "It's exactly what Jade did!"

Mickey's face went pale. "What? That's impossible. How could two people make the exact same design out of team jerseys?"

"It's not *exact*—but it's really close," South said. "I just saw Jade coming up the stairs wearing her version. It's the same idea you had: a long ruffled skirt and a tank top." She checked Jade's Snapchat story. "See? Here she is twirling around in it…and here she is pushing Jake out of the limo…"

Mickey shook her head. This wasn't happening. Not today, the biggest day of her sixth-grade life at

FAB. Jade's design was incredibly similar to hers. It didn't have quite as much length or volume, but there were layers upon layers of jersey scraps used to make tiers of ruffles. And the bodice was the same black tank that Jade had bead-dazzled.

"I have to do something," Mickey said, grabbing her backpack and sewing kit. "I have to change it."

"Now? With ten minutes before class starts?" South exclaimed.

Mickey dug in her bag for something, anything, she could add to make it different. Her hands found a few baseball caps she hadn't used and was planning to return to the scrap box.

"This! This will have to do!" She whipped out a pair of scissors and sliced off the back of the cap. Then she stacked them to make a petal-like shoulder detail on her tank-top shoulders. She hand-sewed fast and furiously and was just finishing up when Jade strolled in.

She froze in her steps when she saw Mickey's design. "You copied me!" she shrieked.

"I copied *you*?" Mickey fired back. "I showed my sketch to Mr. Kaye long before you ever came up with your design. And you were mad that he liked it."

"I don't need to steal anyone's work." Jade sniffed. "People imitate me…not vice versa."

"There's no sense in fighting over it." Jake jumped in between them. "What's done is done."

Gabriel walked in the room next. "Whoa!" he gasped, seeing both Mickey's and Jade's dresses. "Can you say 'hashtag twinning'?"

Jade's face turned red, and Mickey swore she saw steam coming out of her rival ears. "If I get a bad grade because of you…" she said, pointing a finger in Mickey's face.

Mars was the last person to arrive in the studio and gave Mickey's dress form a quick once-over. "I love it," she told Mickey. Then she looked at Jade's. "Um, ditto?"

Mickey took her seat and rested her head in

her hands. This was not going the way she had hoped.

Mr. Kaye arrived right on time and began pulling items out of his briefcase. He took out his grade book and a red pen.

"I hate that pen," Gabriel whispered to Mickey. "It's evil."

"Who wants to present first?" their teacher asked, flipping through the pages of the book.

Mickey gulped. *Maybe he won't notice how similar my dress is to Jade's?* Then she thought again: *Who am I kidding? Mr. Kaye misses nothing!*

She raised her hand high in the air, and so did Jade.

"Ooh, ooh! Me, me!" Jade pleaded.

Mickey stood up. No way was Jade going to wow Mr. Kaye and make her design look like an imitation! "No, me!" she said. "I'd like to go first."

"Oh, I bet you would!" Jade said through gritted teeth.

Mr. Kaye looked over the tops of his reading glasses and suddenly saw what the two girls were arguing over.

"My word! What happened here?" he asked, flabbergasted. "Why are your two final projects so similar?"

"Because she copied me!" Jade shouted.

"In your dreams!" Mickey yelled back. "Mr.

Kaye saw my sketch, and this was it. I was making this gown all along."

"True, true," he remarked. "But did you show your sketch to anyone else?"

Mickey shook her head. "No. No one. Not even my mom."

"Then Jade couldn't have copied you, could she?" he asked her.

"I guess not?" Mickey considered.

Mr. Kaye took off his glasses and rubbed his temples. "This is one of those rare cases where brilliant minds think alike," he said. "Mickey, you made a ball gown, and, Jade, you did a high-low dress—both with the same ruffled texture and materials. But this…" He suddenly walked toward Mickey's dress form. "These shoulder embellishments are ingenious! Are these made from baseball caps?"

Mickey nodded. "I just stuck them on at the last minute so I wouldn't have the exact same look as Jade."

"Good heavens, this was a split-second addition?" he gushed. "It's genius!"

Mickey silently breathed a sigh of relief. She hoped that meant she had earned an A.

The rest of the class each presented their looks: Mars had created a soccer T-shirt dress with an intricate collar made from silver referee whistles.

South had cropped a sweatshirt and added fringe at the bottom from a pair of pom-poms; then she'd created a pencil skirt out of the legs of track shorts stitched together. Gabriel was super proud of his look as well: a wrap dress embellished with assorted letters and numbers he'd pulled off team uniforms.

"Clever," Mr. Kaye said, observing his workmanship. "You created your own textile. And well done on the execution. The stitching is flawless." Gabriel beamed. He was sure to get a passing grade this year—maybe even an A.

Mr. Kaye sat back down at his desk and tapped his pen against his chin. "I have a very difficult decision to make," he said slowly. "You see, not only will the winner of this final project receive an A in my class, but a bonus as well."

A bonus? Mickey liked the sound of that! Just last semester, Mr. Kaye had taken his top students—including her and JC—to Paris to compete against other budding young designers. Maybe he was planning a trip to Madrid…or Milan…or even LA Fashion Week!

"I suppose I should consider the designer with the most photogenic work," he said.

"If you mean who could be on a magazine cover, that would be me," Jade insisted, twirling in her design. "I'm always being photographed by paparazzi, and my mom has had me model several of her looks in *Teen Vogue*."

"Then you don't need a bonus," Mars whispered. "Let someone else have a chance!"

Mr. Kaye walked over once again to Mickey's gown. "I know you have the wherewithal," he said. "But I'm not sure about the courage and confidence."

Mickey shrugged. She had no idea what he was talking about. But if confidence was what he wanted…

"I can do it—whatever *it* is," she told her teacher. "I know I can. I've come such a long way this year, and I really believe in myself and my talent. Please give me the chance to prove it to you!"

Mr. Kaye nodded. "Fine. Mackenzie, meet me in my office fourth period."

Jade stamped her feet. "That's not fair!" she pouted. "I did the same design."

Yes, Mickey thought to herself with a smile, but I did it better!

★ Lights, Camera, Fashion ★

When Mickey reported to Mr. Kaye's office, she was surprised to find JC already seated inside. He waved and gave her a thumbs-up.

"Yes! You rocked your presentation!" her bestie said. "Nice work, Mick."

"Nice work from both of you," Mr. Kaye interrupted. "Ms. Rollings was quite impressed with your final project, young man."

JC leaned back in the chair. "Yeah, it was

pretty spot-on," he joked. "Get it? Dalmatian spots?"

Mr. Kaye scowled. The only one allowed to make fashion puns was him. "I've asked you both here today because FAB has a fantastic opportunity," he continued. "I've been asked to send two of my top students to audition for *Assignment: Fashion Jr.* Are you familiar with the show?"

JC leaped to his feet. "Familiar? Are you kidding me? I can recite every episode by heart! I'm a super fanboy!"

Mr. Kaye looked at Mickey. "And you?"

"Well, I like it a lot," she said. "And I watch it every week. But sometimes I don't agree with the judges. I mean, everyone is entitled to their own fashion opinions, right?"

"I feel faint," JC said, hyperventilating. "I'm gonna be on *Assignment: Fashion*." He offered Mickey his arm. "Pinch me. Please!"

"You understand this is only an *audition*," Mr. Kaye repeated. "You have to do the work and prove yourselves to the judges. It's a foot in the door but no guarantee."

"An audition?" Mickey asked. She pictured herself having to sing and tap-dance for the show's producer and host Helga Floom.

"You will bring your final project and present it to the judges. They will ask you a few questions about yourselves as students and designers. Be honest, be smart, and be sure of yourselves. They are looking for twelve kids to compete on a one-episode junior challenge."

Mickey knew it was a huge long shot they'd choose her. JC knew the show inside and out and had a much better chance. But still, it was pretty amazing that Mr. Kaye had picked her.

JC finally recovered from his excitement. "Don't worry, Mick. I'll give you a crash course in all things *Assignment: Fashion*," he whispered to her. "We'll both get on the show and become huge TV stars!"

Mickey smiled. She didn't care about being a star; she cared about her work being seen.

"Did I mention the prize if you win *Assignment: Fashion Jr.*?" Mr. Kaye asked, checking his notes.

"No," JC said. "What is it? A complete sewing studio from Singer? A spread in *Teen Style* magazine? Five hundred dollars toward starting your own label?"

Mr. Kaye stared. "You really do know the show quite well, don't you?" he asked JC. "Yes, all those things. But it's actually five thousand dollars."

Mickey gasped. Five thousand dollars! She could take her mom and Aunt Olive on an amazing summer vacation with that money! Somewhere exotic— like Hawaii, where she'd always dreamed of going. The pineapple pancakes must be amazing there…

"I could afford to redesign Madonna's room with that money. She's been wanting a canopy dog bed," JC said.

Mickey rolled her eyes. Was that the best thing he could think of to spend his money on? His dog?

"Don't count your cash before your collection," Mr. Kaye warned him. "There's a long way to go before winning—like getting on the show first."

JC stood up and yanked Mickey to her feet with him. "Not a prob," he assured FAB's esteemed design department head. "We won't let you down."

Mr. Kaye raised an eyebrow. "I hope not."

Guess Who's in the Green Room?

The set for *Assignment: Fashion* was a lot larger with many more moving parts than appeared on TV. It was housed on two floors in a university in the New York City Fashion District. There was the sewing room with rows upon rows of machines and work stations; a hair room with blow-dryers, curling irons, and shelves of styling products; a makeup room with hundreds of cosmetics and brushes neatly laid out at mirrored tables; and of course, the runway and judges' panel—a long stage with three swiveling seats at the side.

Mickey and JC reported bright and early on a Saturday morning for the screening process and took a look around before checking in.

"If anyone asks, we're lost," he told her. "I just gotta be in the room where it happens!" He sat down in a judge's seat. "Helga sits here." He sighed heavily. "I'm in Helga's throne."

Mickey shook her head. Getting JC to focus and not act all fanboy wasn't easy. "We better get to the green room before they give away our spots," she said, pulling him along with her.

Seated in the green room—which was really bright pink—were more than two dozen middle-school kids clutching garment bags, sketchbooks, and sewing kits.

"There are a lot of people auditioning," Mickey said, looking around.

"Are you kidding? This is just one day," JC informed her. "They've been auditioning for at least a month—this many kids each day. The competition is fierce."

Mickey gulped. She felt her chances getting smaller and smaller.

"Okay, follow my lead," JC instructed her. "We're not about to sit here all day."

He walked up to the woman who looked like she was in charge. She had dark hair pinned back in a severe bun and was carrying a clipboard.

"Pardon me," he began. "We are the representatives from FAB. You'll want to make sure we're at the top of the list and get to meet with the judges right away."

The woman didn't flinch. "What's a FAB?"

"Are you kidding me?" JC screeched, but Mickey quickly put her hand over his mouth.

"It's our middle school. We should be under Mackenzie Williams and Javen Cumberland."

The woman ran her finger down the sheet. "Yes, I have you." She wrote two numbers on stickers. "Put these on. That's how the judges will refer to you."

Mickey looked at hers: number 24. JC was 8.

"Have a seat." The woman motioned to a couch in the corner. "It's gonna be a while."

Three hours later, they were still sitting and waiting. No one was speaking to anyone else. They were all too nervous or bored. One boy was snoring in the corner, and a girl was polishing her nails.

"I bet he has an amazing portfolio." Mickey pointed to a boy who was wearing a yellow tie, a purple shirt, and orange high-top sneakers. "He looks like he has a lot of personal style."

JC wasn't listening or even attempting to get to know anyone. Friendly was not an option; this was war.

"Unbelievable!" He pouted. "They're taking two kids an hour. At this rate, we'll be here till Christmas!"

Mickey chuckled. "Not quite. But maybe till dinnertime. And you're getting hangry already."

She handed him a snack that Aunt Olive had packed.

"What is this?" JC asked, examining the strange green oval.

"Kale cookies," Mickey answered. "They're not as bad as you'd think."

JC wrinkled his nose. "I have one of Madonna's doggie biscuits in my bag. I'd rather eat that."

Just then, the woman with the clipboard walked into the room. "I need numbers eight and nine," she said.

Mickey shoved JC. "That's you! You're up!"

JC bowed his head as if he was saying a little prayer. Mickey patted him on the back. "You got this," she said. "Go work your JC magic."

Her friend took a deep breath, rose from his seat, and followed the woman out of the room, never looking back.

Mickey figured with a last name starting with *W*, she'd be the last one to audition. So she kicked her feet up on the table and rested her head on the couch pillows.

The boy in the yellow tie suddenly walked over and took a seat next to her.

"Hey," he said simply.

"Hey," Mickey replied. She wasn't sure how JC would feel about her fraternizing with the competition, but he seemed nice enough. And he had dark wavy hair and sparkly blue eyes…

"I'm Jonah Zimm."

"Zimm," Mickey said. "Your name starts with a Z."

Jonah smiled. "The girl can spell!"

"No! I mean, I'm Mickey Williams."

"Oh, a *W*," the boy said. "So we're probably the last two to be seen today." He pointed to his sticker. "I'm number twenty-five, right after you."

Mickey nodded. It was nice to know she wasn't going to be sitting here all alone when everyone else was done. "What school do you go to? I'm at FAB," she said proudly.

"You mean fashion school? None. I'm self-taught. Well, actually my grandma taught me how to sew. I made this shirt and tie."

Mickey looked at the intricate black stitching on the cuffs and collar of his shirt. It was flawless. "You did this?" she said, taking his hand to get a better look at the cuff.

Jonah grinned. "Yeah, I did. It's kinda my thing. I'm all about the details."

"Impressive," she said. "My teacher Mr. Kaye would be wowed."

"Ya think?" Jonah asked. "I've always wanted to go to FAB, but my parents don't think fashion is a serious career choice. They're both lawyers. They want me to be a litigator or a judge or something."

"And you want to be a designer?" Mickey asked.

"More than anything—the next Karl Lagerfeld, Isaac Mizrahi, or Zac Posen. I'm going to run my own billion-dollar fashion empire! I have sketchbooks just filled with ideas. I figure if I can get on this show and win it, maybe my family will take me seriously."

"Can I see some of your sketches?" Mickey asked.

Jonah obliged, taking out a book from his messenger bag. "See this one? I call it 'Moon River.' I want to create a white fabric with a holed Swiss cheese look, drape it into a goddess gown with a long flowing train, and pair it with moon boots that I design to match."

"You make footwear too?" Mickey asked. "That's amazing."

"Well, you have to have accessories to fulfill the vision, you know?"

Mickey *did* know. It was why she made sure her shoes, tights, hat, bag, and even hair highlights worked with her outfit every morning.

"And this one is made from seaweed," he said, flipping the page.

"Nuh-uh! Real seaweed?"

Jonah nodded. "It's an eco-friendly material… fabric from the ocean. I read about it. One day I'll make a mermaid-tail evening gown out of it in a vibrant emerald green."

Wow, Mickey thought. That put her cabbage T-shirt to shame!

"I think you're really talented, Jonah," Mickey said. "I'm sure the judges will love your work."

"Who knows?" he said, putting his feet up next to hers on the table. "I mean, you never know what they're looking for." He pointed to a girl coming into the room, dressed in head-to-toe pink. "It could be her."

Mickey sat straight up and stared. She'd know that rhinestone tiara headband anywhere!

Meet and Greet

"Jade!" Mickey whispered, pulling a couch pillow in front of her face. "Quick, hide me!"

"You know her?" Jonah asked.

"Unfortunately," Mickey replied. "She goes to my school."

"Well, that explains the great sense of style…" He was referring to her faux fur jacket and Chanel backpack, which she'd casually slung over one shoulder. "What's with the tiara? Is she royalty or something?"

"Oh, she's *something*, all right," Mickey said.

"And somehow she's managed to worm her way into this audition."

"Mickey," Jade said, strolling over. "Fancy meeting you here."

Mickey came out from hiding. "What are you doing here? Mr. Kaye didn't invite you."

Jonah stood up and offered his hand. "I'm Jonah. And you are?"

"Disgusted," Jade replied with a sigh, "by the horrific lack of talent represented here. My mother will be appalled."

"Your mother?" Jonah asked.

Mickey held up her hand. "Don't go there. You'll be sorry."

"Why yes!" Jade seized the opportunity to brag. "My mother is Bridget Lee, the fabulously famous fashion designer—and in fact, one of Helga's dearest friends."

Mickey raised an eyebrow. "Let me get this straight. Your mom is besties with one of the judges, and you're competing? How is that fair?"

"I didn't say I was competing." Jade smiled slyly. "I'm just helping with the screening process. Helga values my opinion."

"Oh!" Jonah said, oozing charm. "Of course she does! Who wouldn't? So you can put in a good word for me, right?" He winked. "Would ya, could ya?"

"Perhaps," Jade said. "I did just tell the judges

not to seriously consider your little bowwow boyfriend, Mickey."

Mickey leaped to her feet. "You did not! Jade, that's horrible! JC worked so hard for this, and he's crazy talented!"

"Crazy, yes. Talented? Not so sure." Jade looked around the room, surveying the remaining candidates. "But then again, compared to this sad bunch…"

"Let the judges make up their own minds," Mickey pleaded with her. "Please!"

Jade grinned. "So let me get this straight. You don't want me to tell Helga to choose you and not JC?"

Mickey's face went pale. Was Jade actually suggesting she sell out her best friend for a place on the show? JC would be devastated—crushed! He ate, slept, and breathed *Assignment Fashion*. She couldn't let Jade take that away from him, even if it meant destroying her only chances.

"Just one word, and JC is history…and you're in," Jade baited her. "Of course, he'd probably never speak to you again…"

So that was her game! She wanted to ensure that Mickey and JC were no longer friends. "No," Mickey insisted. "Don't say anything."

Jonah took Jade by the arm. "Well, I'm okay with you saying anything you want about *me* to the judges." He gazed into her eyes. "So is your mom as pretty as you are?"

Jade blushed. "Flattery will get you everywhere."

Mickey pretended to gag. Couldn't Jade see that Jonah was only flirting with her to get ahead in the competition? But then again, he did seem a little interested.

"What did you say your name was? Sapphire? Ruby?" he asked.

"Jade," she said, giggling.

"Oh, that's not a precious enough stone for you! Your mom should have named you Diamond."

Mickey groaned. "I just ate a kale cookie, and you people are making me sick."

Jade took Jonah's arm. "You're number twenty-five. That's the last one to audition," she noted. "We can't have that!" She peeled the sticker off his shirt and crumpled it into a ball. "No need to wait that long. Come with me, and I'll introduce you to Helga."

"Maybe we can grab lunch too?" Jonah offered. "I'd love to hear all about you."

"You would?" Jade asked, batting her eyelashes. "There's so much to tell!"

As they walked toward the green room door, Jonah glanced over his shoulder and winked at Mickey. Then he put his fingers to his lip to signal her to keep quiet.

Mickey sank back into the sofa. Great, she thought. Now she was back to being last in line, and Jade was surely going to sabotage her chances with the judges before she ever even got her turn. And poor JC—he didn't stand a chance. Not with Jade meddling. They'd both go home empty-handed. But at least they'd do it together.

"Mackenzie Williams?" The woman with the clipboard stuck her head back inside the green room door.

Mickey snapped to attention. "Yes! That's me."

"You're up."

Mickey looked around the room at all the other students who had numbers lower than hers.

"You sure? I'm number twenty-four."

The woman put her hands on her hips. "Would you like a written invitation?"

"No! Coming!" Mickey said, gathering her sketchbook and garment bag.

When she got to the set, she saw that all three judges were seated in their swivel chairs at the side of the runway. Helga was gabbing away to her dynamic duo: Jack Rosen, one of the biggest fashion designers in the world, and Lena Gomez, creative director of *Teen Style* magazine. Then she noticed a fourth figure standing with them: JC!

"Mickey!" JC suddenly waved at her. "Come and meet the gang!"

Mickey couldn't believe it. Helga had her arm around him!

"This is my BFF Mickey," JC said, introducing her. "And Mick, these are Helga, Jack, and Lena."

Helga smiled, flashing perfect, white supermodel teeth. "JC told us so much about you."

"JC told *you*?" Mickey tried to wrap her brain around what was happening. "I'm sorry… I'm a bit confuzzled."

"In thirteen seasons, we've never quite met anyone like him," Jack explained. "He's a walking encyclopedia of all things *Assignment: Fashion*. Our superfan extraordinaire."

"I think we need to hire you as a consultant," Helga chimed in. "You know more than I do."

JC nodded. "Go ahead. Ask me anything. Anything."

Lena clapped her hands together: "Who was the winner of season two's avant-garde challenge?"

"Easy!" JC said. "Finola Hierro. She made those cool yoga pants out of the *Sunday Times*."

"Yes!" Jack cheered. "The extra, extra paper challenge! I loved that one."

"Okay… Here's a bonus question," Helga piped up. "Who accidentally sent his model down the runway in a pair of trousers without a zipper?"

"Oh, so simple!" JC boasted. "Liam Weill,

season four semifinals. He didn't have a zipper that matched his gold brocade suit, so he sewed his model into the trousers and had to cut her out. Awkward!"

"Yaaaaaas!" Jack cheered. "You nailed that one!"

"And he stitched that one!" JC shouted back, high-fiving him.

Mickey stood there, positively speechless. So much for Jade ruining JC's chances. The judges loved him!

"So, Mick." JC interrupted the merriment. "Helga and I were just chatting, and I told her you're one of the most original, creative designers at FAB. Show her your stuff."

Mickey stood there, frozen and starstruck.

"Mick," JC repeated, elbowing her. "Show the judges your stuff. Work with me, here!"

Mickey nodded and unzipped her garment bag. Jack Rosen's face lit up. "Are those team jerseys?" he asked.

Mickey gulped. "Yes, sir."

"Remarkable," Lena gushed. "So editorial. I could easily see this on the pages of *Teen Style* magazine."

"Are you kidding?" Helga said. "I could see it on me—on a red carpet. I love it."

"You do?" Mickey asked, still stunned.

"Absolutely!" Helga replied. "JC, you were right. Definite *Assignment: Fashion Jr.* material."

"Did I tell ya or did I tell ya, Helg?" JC said. "I would never steer you guys wrong."

"So we're agreed?" Jack said, conferring with his fellow judges. Both women nodded.

"JC and Mickey, welcome to the show!"

8

★ Nothing Stays the Same ★

All the way on the walk home from the audition, Mickey tried to process what she'd just witnessed. It hadn't even begun to sink in that she was about to compete on TV's top fashion reality show.

"So Jade didn't sabotage us?" she asked JC. "She didn't tell her mom not to whisper in Helga's ear to kick us out?"

"If she did, it doesn't matter," JC explained.

"Helga still runs the show. She's the executive producer. I one-upped Jade."

"And Helga is your new BFF?" Mickey giggled.

JC shrugged. "Well, we're close and all—but you're still my BFF, Mick," he said. "Let's just say she comes in a close second."

"I'll take it," Mickey said. "But this whole thing is surreal."

"I know, right?" JC exclaimed. "I was telling Helga how it was my dream to be on *Assignment: Fashion*, and the next thing I knew, she was quizzing me and cracking up at my jokes."

"You're incredible, JC," Mickey said. "Only you!"

"Just because we're on the show doesn't mean we're going to win," JC reminded her. "I hate to be Debbie Downer here, but there are ten other serious contenders."

"But none of them have your encyclopedic knowledge," Mickey reminded him.

"Or your creativity," he replied. "Okay, I take it back. Those other kids should be scared. We're the real deal."

Mickey chuckled. "We are, aren't we?" she said, linking arms with him as they walked through the crowded Midtown streets.

JC stopped in his tracks. "Can we just make a promise to each other, Mick?"

"Sure. Anything."

"No matter what happens, no matter how ugly or fierce this competition gets, we're BFFFs: best fashion friends forever."

Mickey held up her pinkie. "I swear it."

"Phew, now I feel better," JC said, and resumed their walk. "Because in season five, Bella and Ivan were besties and wound up hating each other's guts over the 'No Business Like Snow Business' challenge. The snowflakes were flying, and it was not pretty…"

Mickey shrugged. "Sounds pretty. If you feel the urge to throw snowflakes at me, feel free," she said.

JC shook his head. "Nuh-uh. Trust me, that was one of the biggest fights ever in *Assignment: Fashion* history. To this day, Bella and Ivan are on the outs. It's tragic!"

"Well, I'm not Bella, and you're not Ivan," Mickey insisted.

"Gosh, I hope not." JC shuddered. "He had the worst style ever—all black and goth, not a pink or polka dot to be found. I could never!"

When Mickey arrived home, Olive already had dinner set on the table.

"You smelled my tofu risotto!" Olive said, as Mickey opened the door.

"Yum." Mickey tried to be kind. Her aunt was always experimenting with strange vegan dishes.

"And I made coconut date bites for dessert to celebrate."

Mickey looked puzzled. "Celebrate what?"

"You getting on *Assignment: Fashion*. Your mom told me you called her on the way home with the news."

"Aw, I wanted to tell you myself!" Mickey whined.

"And my promotion…kind of," Olive said slowly. "My boss asked me to head up the entire paralegal department at Simpson Zimm Rose Lattanzi Partners. The executive director job."

Mickey threw her arms around her aunt's waist. "Oh, Aunt Olive. That's wonderful! I'm so happy for you! It's what you've wanted for so long!" Then she realized Olive didn't look all that happy. "Doesn't it mean a big raise? And your own big office with a view?"

"Yes, yes, it does," Olive said, pulling out a chair for Mickey to take a seat. "Which is why it's hard for me to turn it down."

"Turn it down? Why would you ever do that?"

Olive sighed. "Because it would also mean relocating to the Los Angeles office," she answered.

Mickey let the words sink in. "You mean, you couldn't live here in New York anymore? *We* couldn't live here in New York anymore? And I couldn't go to FAB anymore?"

Olive nodded. "I would never ask you to leave your school, Mackenzie. I know how much it means to you."

Mickey knew that only a few short months ago, Olive would have done practically anything to earn this promotion—and she would have been on the first flight to California. She took great pride in her job and always said how much she wanted an executive position. She'd been a loyal employee for twenty years.

But now, she was willing to throw everything away...for Mickey.

"You can't turn it down," Mickey insisted, regretting the words the instant they came out of her mouth. "I...I'll just have to leave FAB and go back home to Philly."

"I already spoke to your mother. We're not going to allow that to happen. She wanted to give up her job and come here to live with you, but I said I'd be just fine staying where I was."

"No way!" Mickey cried. "Mom can't give up her job, and neither can you—not for me."

"We love you." Olive smiled. "And when you love someone, you make sacrifices."

Mickey's eyes filled with tears. "But not this. It's too much. I can't ruin your life!"

Olive reached across the table and took her hand. "Mackenzie, six months ago you came to live with me, and you made my life so much better than it ever was. I never had someone to take care of before. Except Percy…" She pointed to her yellow parakeet chirping away in its cage. "And he bites so that doesn't count."

"I love you too, Aunt Olive," Mickey said. "Which is why I can't let you do this!"

"I told my boss I'd have an answer for him in a week after I talked it over with my family," Olive added. "Your mom and I made the decision tonight, and I think it's the right one."

"No, it's not! Not for you!" Mickey felt the tears streaming down her face. "You can't give up your dream, Aunt Olive! I won't let you!" She ran into her room and shut the door behind her. How had this day gone so suddenly wrong? One minute, she was about to be on *Assignment: Fashion Jr.* And the next…she was leaving NYC, FAB, and JC for good.

The producers of *Assignment: Fashion Jr.* emailed the twelve contestants instructions for the upcoming week of filming. They would be excused from school so they could participate fully in the show. There would be personal on-camera interviews, B-roll shots of them working in the sewing studio, draping their dress forms, and gathering materials, then the live runway show the next day where the winner and three runners-up would be chosen to win prizes.

Mickey couldn't concentrate on reading the complicated instructions. She was too busy thinking about Aunt Olive. When her cell phone rang, she knew it would be JC, already having read the email several times and strategizing.

"Okay," he said as soon as she picked up. "I

think they're going to do an unconventional challenge—some strange materials that you would never think to use in fashion, but you have to or else."

"Uh-huh," Mickey said absentmindedly.

"You have to be prepared," JC continued. "Expect full-on crazy, like gathering your material from a cafeteria, a party store, a construction site. They've done 'em all."

"Right," Mickey replied. "No school this week...*Assignment: Fashion.*"

"Are you even listening to me?" JC asked, growing impatient. "You have to plan for this, Mickey. You don't have a lot of time to think, much less sketch, so you have to have your head in the game. I think yours is somewhere else."

Mickey sighed. "My aunt can't leave New York City because of me," she said.

"Yeah, you live with her. Nothing new there."

"You don't understand, JC. She has this amazing opportunity to work in California in this job she's always dreamed of, and she has to say no because she's stuck with me."

JC thought for a second. "Well, what's the alternative? Go back to unfashionable Philly and your old life?"

Mickey gulped. It really didn't sound appealing.

"Mickey, you're not considering…" JC began.

"I dunno. Maybe. I mean, I've had a whole year here at FAB. It's been great…"

"And it's not ending!" JC insisted. "You can't leave. We'll have to figure something else out. I'm not letting my best friend bail on me."

Mickey sighed. If only there was another solution. "Aunt Olive gave me the chance to follow my dreams. How can I take hers away from her?"

"Well, now you've been given a chance on *Assignment: Fashion*, which you're about to blow!" JC scolded her. "Mickey, get through the next two days, impress the judges, and we'll figure the rest out later. Okay?"

"Okay," Mickey said. "I'll try."

"You'll do more than just try," JC instructed her. "You'll have a game plan, no matter what challenge they throw at you. As soon as you hear what the theme is, you have to react with lightning-quick reflexes."

"JC, don't you think you're overthinking this a bit?"

"No such thing!" he shot back. "I intend to spend the entire night analyzing every challenge the show has ever done—and what the winning designs were."

"I think I'll wing it," Mickey said. "I do much better when I'm spontaneous. It'll just come to me."

"Or it won't," JC warned her. "And you'll be

standing there, staring into space, while everyone else is stitching up a storm. But hey, I tried to help you out…"

"You did, JC, and I appreciate it," she said. "But I'll take my chances."

"Fine, just promise me you won't worry about your aunt until after the show is over," JC pleaded with her. "It's two days, Mickey. A lot can change in a day."

Poker Face

JC marched into the *Assignment: Fashion* studios with not even a glance at his fellow competitors. He pulled Mickey along by the hand.

"Don't look any of them in the eye. You'll give it away."

"Give what away?" Mickey asked.

"Your game plan. Keep a perfect poker face. Don't tip your hand."

Mickey noticed a boy waving to her from across the studio set.

"Hey! *W* girl!" he called.

"*Z* boy!" Mickey shouted back. So Jonah had actually gotten Jade to help him secure a spot on the show! Or maybe he was really *that* good on his own.

"Did you not hear what I said?" JC scolded her. "No contact. No chitchatting with *Z* boy or whatever his name is."

"Jonah," Mickey corrected him. "And he's coming over to chitchat right now."

JC glared at him. "Sorry, she can't talk." He jumped between them. "Mickey's on a mission. Gotta go, Joe…"

He escorted her to the opposite side of the studio, as far away from Jonah as they could get.

"JC, that was rude. He was trying to be friendly."

"He was trying to get you to spill your secrets," JC replied.

"I don't have any secrets," Mickey protested.

"This is a battlefield, Mick, and it's war. Don't trust anyone."

"Not even you?" Mickey teased.

"Not even me. Unless I say so."

Mickey tried not to laugh. "Okay, so what do we do?"

"We scope out the studio, pick the best tables with the best lighting, and set up camp."

Mickey placed her sewing kit—a small tackle box filled with needles, pins, scissors, and buttons—on a wooden table in the center of the room. "This looks like a good spot."

"In the center? Where everyone can see you and spy on your work?" JC gasped. He grabbed her kit and placed it next to his—on a table tucked into the back corner of the studio. "You don't want anyone to be able to watch what you're doing and steal your ideas."

Mickey rolled her eyes; JC was getting a little carried away.

"And that's all you brought? That itty-bitty tackle box?" he asked her.

"Yeah," Mickey replied. "What else would I need?"

JC unpacked the contents of his rolling backpack, messenger bag, and dog tote. There was no Madonna in it today—just several dozen zippers, assorted trim, buttons, sequins, studs, and beads, and at least a hundred different spools of thread.

"Are you planning on sewing outfits for the entire crew?" Mickey exclaimed. "You don't need all of this."

"I do. I have studied every show, and I have prepared for every possibility." He held up a purple zipper. "If the challenge involves eggplants, I'm totally covered."

"Fashion designers of the future!" Helga called

as she strutted into the studio. The supermodel was dressed in a tight purple dress and high heels.

"See?" JC whispered to Mickey. "She likes purple. That zipper will come in handy."

"Welcome to *Assignment: Fashion Jr.*," Helga continued. "We're so excited to have you all here and see what you can do. You've already wowed us with your expertise."

JC beamed. "She means me."

"Your challenge will be a little ruff, so make sure you have claws out," she said. "And if you think something's fishy…you're right!"

JC's face suddenly went white. "Oh no. They've never done that before…"

"Done what?" Mickey asked.

"You will be competing in an unconventional challenge, and your materials will come from Pet Emporium!" Helga announced.

Mickey thought JC would be thrilled—dogs were his thing! Instead, he looked as pale as a ghost.

"I have nothing," he said, devastated. "No plan. No idea. I didn't prepare for this at all, and now I'm doomed."

"Contestants, we will be leaving in five minutes. All the materials you use to create your looks must come from Pet Emporium—no exceptions. You have a fifty-dollar budget to spend, and today and part of tomorrow to create your looks. Good luck!" Helga pointed to the cameras, already shooting away. "And everything will be captured for our TV audiences!"

JC looked like he was going to faint. "Doomed. Doomed. Doomed," he said over and over.

Mickey seized him by the shoulders and shook him. There was no other way to snap him out of it. "Get a grip on yourself!" she shouted. "And get it fast!" She noticed a cameraman zooming in on her. Her little outburst probably made for great TV.

"Um, hi out there, millions of people watching this," she said, waving. "I'm Mickey and this is JC."

She turned her friend to face the camera. "What do you want to tell the viewers, JC?"

Suddenly, the color returned to JC's cheeks. "I'm totally excited for this challenge." He perked up as the camera lens came closer. "Because no one knows this show better than I do."

Mickey breathed a huge sigh of relief. JC was back.

"And cut!" the director said, giving him a thumbs-up. "That'll be a nice close-up for you, kid." JC smiled weakly.

"Feeling better?" Mickey asked him.

"I'm a wreck," he confessed. "But I also remembered that in season six, Laverne didn't have a clue what to do for the pizza restaurant unconventional challenge and wound up creating the winning look."

"What did she do?"

"She made a jumpsuit out of pizza aprons," he recalled.

"You mean she winged it," Mickey pointed out.

"Technically, she mozzarella-ed it," JC corrected her. "She used the shredded cheese as fringe on the jumpsuit. It was inspired."

"I know you can do better than that," Mickey encouraged him. "You're always shopping for Madonna in Pet Emporium."

"For biscuits and bones and wee-wee pads." JC groaned. "Not for a fashionable couture look."

"But you know every inch of that store and where things are. You're totally prepared."

JC's face lit up. "You know, you're right. I have a huge advantage. I'm gonna win this!"

She pushed him toward the door. "That's the JC I know and love."

"And the JC who's going to win *Assignment: Fashion Jr.*," he added.

Like I said, Mickey thought to herself, he's *baaaack*!

Ready, Set...Pets!

As soon as they walked through the door of Pet Emporium, JC made a beeline straight for the second aisle where all the cat and dog supplies were kept. "Outta my way!" he bellowed at the other kids.

"Whoa, he's intense, isn't he?" Jonah asked Mickey.

"Ya think?" She laughed.

"Any idea what you're gonna do?" he asked.

Mickey remembered what JC had said: keep a poker face and reveal nothing.

"Nope, just browsing," she replied. "I think I'll head down this aisle."

She found herself surrounded by cages of colorful, chirping birds and endless bags of seed. It reminded her of Percy the parakeet, and of course Aunt Olive, who was an avid bird-watcher.

"I got almost everything," JC said, racing past her with a shopping cart. "Why are you just standing there?"

"I'm thinking," Mickey said.

JC glanced at his watch. "Think quicker! We have only fifteen more minutes." He headed for the register as Mickey scanned the bags of birdseed.

"Interesting," she said out loud.

"What is?" Jonah said, sneaking up behind her. "What do you think of this velour doggie bed? Do you think the material could make for a great bomber jacket?"

"I...I don't know," Mickey said, not wanting to give him any hints or help. JC would kill her!

She picked up an empty basket and began filling it with seed. Then she grabbed some feathered toys in the cat section and a dozen yellow doggie sweaters. Before she checked out, she grabbed a giant rope knot ball and something that looked like a rainbow-colored canvas tunnel—she assumed for cats and dogs to play in.

"Interesting is right," Jonah said, looking over her purchases. "You've got some unusual ideas, *W* girl."

"You must have some too—or the judges wouldn't have picked you," Mickey answered. "Unless you charmed Jade into helping you get a spot."

Jonah flashed a smile. "I am charming, aren't I?" he said. "Thanks for noticing."

"What? Huh?" Mickey stammered. "I never said that." JC was right. She had to watch every word and trust no one!

"For the record, Jade's not my type," Jonah said. "Too uppity. All she wanted to talk about was herself. It got boring pretty fast."

Mickey *really* wanted to ask him what his type was—especially when his blue eyes sparkled at her under the fluorescent lights.

"Mickey!" JC said, crashing his cart into Jonah's. "Let's get a move on...now!"

Jonah smirked. "You usually take orders from this guy?"

"No, she doesn't take orders from anyone," JC answered before Mickey could open her mouth. "Mickey does her own thing."

Mickey shrugged her shoulders. "I kinda do."

"Now *that* is my type," Jonah said, flirting with her. "In case you were wondering."

They were back on the bus in the backseat when JC read Mickey the riot act.

"Are you crazy? He's trying to sabotage you!"

"What? You're nuts. He's just being friendly."

"So he can get to you," JC insisted. "I'm telling you, every *Assignment: Fashion* has a slimy, back-stabbing villain, and that guy is it."

Mickey crossed her arms over her chest. "I don't believe it. I think he's nice."

"Nice? Nice?" JC was trying not to lose his temper. "Did you see that python in the tank at the pet store? It eats cute, fuzzy little mice for lunch."

"So?" Mickey asked.

"So you're the cute, fuzzy little mouse!" JC said, patting Mickey's faux fur vest.

"And you think Jonah's the snake?"

"Don't think," JC answered. "I know. He totally fits the character. They picked him because of it."

"I saw his sketchbook. They picked him because he's really talented," Mickey said.

JC waved his hand in the air dismissively.

"Whatever. I've seen every episode a dozen times, and I'm never wrong."

"Well, you were wrong about the unconventional challenge," Mickey reminded him. Why was she getting so defensive? JC was her friend, not Jonah. But Jonah *was* really cute and kind of fun to talk to…

"Fine," she agreed. "I won't get stuck in a trap."

"Ssssssmart choice," JC hissed in her ear.

Then she noticed the back of Jonah's head seated a few rows in front of her, and her heart did a little flip-flop. She promised herself she'd be careful and mind what JC had told her—but what was the harm in making a new friend?

★ Assignment: Fashion Diva! ★

The crew set the huge digital clock on the studio wall to count down eight hours.

"They're not kidding, are they?" Mickey said. "When they say one day for your challenge, they mean it."

"They'll stop it somewhere around nine p.m. tonight," JC explained. "That it resumes at eight a.m. tomorrow. We'll have another three or four hours, then it's time to show on the runway, whether your look is finished or not."

A pretty blond girl tapped JC on the shoulder. "You seem really knowledgeable," she said. "Maybe you can give me a few pointers. I'm from Switzerland, and I've only seen the show once or twice."

"Not now, not ever!" JC snapped at her.

"He left his manners at home." Mickey tried to apologize.

Soon every competitor in the room figured out they had to keep their distance—or JC would rip their heads off.

He was setting up his needles and threads when Mickey peered over his shoulder.

"No spying!" he shouted, throwing a sheet of muslin over the table to cover his patterns.

"JC, it's me," Mickey said. "You don't mean me."

"I do," he said, regaining his composure. "I'm sorry, Mick, but you stay in your corner, and I'll stay in mine."

This was getting ridiculous! JC was out of control and acting like a total design diva! But there was nothing she could do about it. The clock was ticking, and she had her own design to worry about.

She carefully sketched out her vision in her notebook: a yellow halter sweater, a rainbow patterned mini hoop skirt, and a cropped jacket "beaded" with birdseed. She'd use the colorful rope from the ball to trim the cuffs and collar, and the feathers on the cat toys would be a colorful accent—maybe a headpiece. She hoped that the judges would like it. She winced as she imagined what Helga might say: "That look is for the birds!"

"Do you have an extra thimble?" the blond girl asked her.

Mickey dug in her sewing kit and pulled one out. "Sure, here ya go."

"That's so nice of you. Not many kids here are nice."

"I think they're just busy and focused," Mickey

explained. She was sure she was referring to JC. "There's a lot of pressure."

The girl shrugged. "I'm just happy to be here. I go to a design school in Zurich. It's very different."

"I can imagine!" Mickey said. "Wait, no, I can't! I've never been to Switzerland. It must be beautiful."

"It is," the girl explained. "I miss it. But my parents think it's better for me to study fashion here in the United States."

Mickey nodded. "Well, I'm kind of away from my home too. I live in Philly, but I stay here in New York with my aunt so I can go to FAB."

"My name is Lara," the girl said.

"I'm Mickey. Nice to meet you."

"Can I ask you one more question, Mickey?" Lara asked shyly. "Can you look at my sketch and tell me if you think it's okay?"

Mickey looked around the room, making sure JC wasn't watching her. He'd flip out if he saw her offering help to another competitor. She took the sketch from Lara and studied it. It was beautifully drawn and brilliantly conceived.

"Is this coat made out of canvas?" Mickey asked her.

"Actually, it's the material the kitties scratch their claws on," Lara replied. "I don't know what you call it."

"Oh my gosh, that's amazing," Mickey said,

whistling through her teeth. "A scratching post! But it must be so hard to sew with this material! Like stitching a rug, not a trench coat."

"I will have to do it all by hand, which is why I needed your thimble. Thank you."

Mickey smiled. JC wasn't kidding—the competition was fierce.

"Good luck, Lara," Mickey called after her. The clock now had less than seven hours left— and she had to get down to business.

The time seemed to fly by, and before the students

knew it, it was 9:00 p.m. and Helga was bouncing back into the workroom and telling them to pack up their work for the day.

"You'll have tomorrow to fit your models, meet with your hair and makeup stylists, and get everything ready for the runway."

"She says that like it's easy," Jonah groaned. "I'm not even halfway done with my design."

"Me neither," Mickey said, sighing. She looked over at JC, who was meticulously placing his scissors in a neat line on his workstation.

"You're quiet," Mickey said. "How's it going?"

"Fine, fine," JC said. But Mickey knew her bestie. He wasn't *fine* or anything close to it. If he were, he would be dancing around, humming a Madonna song.

"How's your design coming along?"

"Fine, fine," JC said again.

"JC…" Mickey leaned in to whisper. "If you're freaking out, you can tell me. I can help."

"I don't want your help, Mickey," he insisted. "I don't want anybody's help."

"I'm not just anybody," Mickey replied. "I'm your best friend."

"Then mind your own bceswax," JC shot back.

Mickey tried not to take JC's rudeness personally. He was clearly under a lot of stress and, like always, would apologize later. But she was worried about him. She decided to sneak a peek at his sketchbook while he went to the sewing room to gather his materials and pack them up.

As she thumbed through the pages, she couldn't believe what she saw: JC was designing a cropped jacket and matching sheath "beaded" with kitty litter.

"You stole my idea!" she said when he returned to his table.

"You looked in my sketchbook without my permission!" JC yelled.

Helga signaled for one of the cameramen to come over. "Make sure you're getting this on film," she said. "Feuding friends!"

"How could you?" Mickey shouted back. "Are you that desperate to win, JC?"

"You know I would never steal another designer's idea! How would I know you were doing something similar?"

"Then how do you explain this?" Mickey demanded, waving his book in the air.

"I don't know!" JC said, wringing his hands. "It's like when Jade had the same ruffled skirt made out of team jerseys as you did. Brilliant minds think alike."

"I don't buy it," Mickey said, storming away. "I think you want this so bad you would do anything—even steal from a friend—to get it. You looked at my sketches, and you won't admit it."

She picked up her bag and left the room, leaving JC at his station, and the rest of the competitors staring with open mouths.

"Wow," Helga said. "That was intense. I can't wait to see what happens tomorrow." Then she turned the rest of the kids. "Night-night! Sleep tight! See you bright and early!"

Runway Redo

When the doors to the *Assignment: Fashion* workroom opened at 8:00 a.m., the students all rushed in to get back to sewing. Mickey saw JC but didn't make eye contact—she was too angry. She had to simply focus on finishing her work and getting it ready for the runway. There was no time to scrap her original design and come up with something different from his. She hoped the judges wouldn't disqualify them both!

"You don't have to worry," JC said, suddenly approaching her table. "I'm not sending my look down the runway."

"What do you mean?" Mickey asked. "You have to. You have nothing else."

"Two similar looks always cancel each other out," he said. "I've seen it happen on several different seasons. There's no use in both of us losing."

"What? You can't quit, JC!"

"I don't have a choice," he replied. He circled Mickey's dress form and examined her jacket, top and skirt. "Your design is better than mine, Mickey. It's more ambitious, more out-of-the-box. It's what the judges love."

"But this show means everything to you!"

"Not everything," JC said. "Your friendship means more. I couldn't sleep last night, knowing how mad you were at me."

"I'm sorry!" Mickey cried. "I know you didn't do it on purpose."

JC tried to manage a joke. "What's done is done. No use crying over spilled kitty litter, right?"

"But what if you didn't have to get rid of your look?" Mickey asked. "What if you change it up a bit."

"What do you mean?" JC asked.

"Think about your Dalmatian-print jumpsuit,"

Mickey suggested. "What if you dyed some of the kitty litter black…"

"…and created a pattern. That's genius. You know what would be even more genius?"

Mickey raised an eyebrow. "What?"

"Leopard spots! A kitty-litter cat print!"

"Wow, cats and not dogs? That's really thinking out of the box for you, JC."

"I know, right?" JC said. "I'm excited!"

Mickey glanced at the clock—the models would be coming in any minute. "I'll help," she volunteered. "If we both work on it, we'll get it done twice as fast."

"You would do that?" JC asked. "For me?"

Mickey smiled. "What are friends for?"

The next few hours were a whirlwind of putting the finishing touches on the outfits, making sure they perfectly fit the models, getting their hair and makeup done, and rehearsing the walk on the runway.

"Head up! Shoulders back," Jonah instructed his model. Mickey admired the gorgeous emerald-green gown he'd made her. The skirt was stiff and sculpted into a bell-like shape.

"That's not your seaweed fabric, is it?" she asked him.

"I wish! It's the green turf used to decorate the

bottom of an aquarium," he said. "And the bodice is a mosaic of aquarium pebbles."

"Wow!" Mickey said. "I would never know it wasn't couture."

"Let's hope the judges agree," Jonah said crossing his fingers, "and that they don't throw me to the sharks."

The contestants and their models made their way to the runway, where Helga, Jack, and Lena were all seated, waiting for the show to begin. The audience had also filed in to watch the competition. Mr. Kaye was front and center along with Jade and her mom. And in the back row, waving at Mickey, was Aunt Olive. The rest of the parents, friends, and fashion insiders filled in the seats.

"Don't pay attention to the crowd," JC advised Mickey. "When you present your look to the judges, it's only you and them. Got it?"

Mickey nodded, but her nerves were on edge. "Just look at the judges, not the people," she repeated back to him.

"And not the cameras either," JC coached her. "You want to look cool and confident—not like a deer caught in the headlights."

"Try to forget a gazillion people around the world will be watching you," Jonah added. "And in my case, a pair of disapproving parents."

JC actually felt a pang of sympathy for him. "Your parents don't want you to be a designer?" he asked. "That's awful. I don't know what I'd do if fashion wasn't an option for me."

"Yeah, well, you're lucky. You have parents and teachers and friends who believe in you. I just have me."

"Not true," Mickey said, resting her hand on his shoulder. "I believe in you."

Jonah smiled. "Really? No one has ever told me that before." He gazed into her eyes.

"Okay, lovebirds, we have a runway to rock," JC said, dragging them both to their seats.

"What? No! We're just friends," Mickey assured him.

"Uh-huh," JC whispered. "Friends who make goo-goo eyes at each other."

She took a seat between the two of them and tried her best to focus. She saw that Lara was biting her nails, and another kid was banging his head on the back of a chair. Everyone was falling apart at the seams!

"You nervous?" Lara asked her.

"Uh-huh," Mickey said. "My knees are knocking."

"Oh." Lara laughed. "I thought those were mine making that noise!"

Helga held up her hand and summoned everyone's attention.

"Ladies and gentleman, welcome to the runway for *Assignment: Fashion Jr.* I am pleased to present the very brightest young designers from around the world, competing today for the title of champion and a five-thousand-dollar scholarship to help jump-start their fashion career. We will also have three runners-up taking home two-thousand dollar, one-thousand-dollar, and five-hundred-dollar scholarships respectively."

She introduced the judges, then cued the lights and music. The models paraded down the runway one by one, wearing each of the contestants' pet store–inspired designs.

JC was wide-eyed, taking it all in. "They're all so good," he whispered to Mickey. "This is going to be a tough choice for the judges." He took out a sheet of paper and began jotting down notes.

"What are you doing?" Mickey asked.

"Figuring out the winners," he said. "It's really pretty logical. I know Helga, Jack, and Lena's voting records over the past thirteen seasons. I know what they like and what they don't. I should be able to get it down to the top five easily."

Jonah leaned over. "Could you maybe put my name down on your list? That's my design coming down the runway now."

JC watched the model walk, pause, turn, and walk again. The green turf gown was a sculptural masterpiece, and the strapless bodice, made from blue, yellow, and purple pebbles, looked more like a piece of art than aquarium supplies.

"I might rank you in the top five," JC said thoughtfully. "You did a great job. The workmanship is flawless, and it shows great creativity. It's right up Jack's alley."

Jonah smiled. "Really? You think so?"

"Oh, he *knows* so," Mickey added.

The next piece down the runway was Lara's trench coat, made entirely of scratch-post fabric. She'd frayed the edges and added a dramatic gold belt, pieced together from lids of cat food cans.

"Okay, that's a definite possibility," JC said. "It's ingenuous."

Each piece that followed was equally clever: a sweater woven out of dog leashes, a blazer made of dog harnesses paired with a hamster-wheel hat, a velour coat crafted from dog beds.

"Ooh, I was thinking of using those," Jonah recalled.

"Don't second-guess yourself," JC warned him.

"Confidence is key when you face those judges. Defend your design!"

Mickey sat up straight as soon as she saw her model waiting in the wings. As her look came down the runway, the judges' faces were blank. She'd done her very best to create a classic jacket, inspired by Chanel, covered with birdseed to create texture and trimmed with rainbow-colored rope for contrast. The top was a simple yellow halter, tucked into a playful hoop mini skirt in rainbow-colored canvas. But her favorite part was the long feathers that the hair stylist had woven into the model's updo. It pulled the entire outfit together.

"It's good, really good," JC told her. He'd written her name on his list and underlined it twice. "Fun, yet fashion forward—a winning combination." But Mickey knew the contest was far from over. She still had to face the judges and explain her motivation.

JC's look was the last down the runway. As the model stepped out into the light, the suit sprung to life. He'd created a pink leopard-print pattern on the kitty litter-bedecked jacket and skirt. And as if that weren't enough, he'd sprinkled it with glitter, so the entire outfit twinkled under the runway lights. As the model reached the judges, she purred like a kitten and peeled off the jacket, revealing a black mesh tank with pink trim.

"What is that made out of?" Jonah asked.

"Kitty carrier!" JC said proudly. "It was a last-minute decision. I winged it."

Jack Rosen almost fell out of his chair, and Lena had a smile on her face the entire time. The only one Mickey couldn't read was Helga. She seemed very, very serious.

"Okay," she said when the last model had returned backstage and the music had stopped. "We will now call some names."

JC grabbed Mickey's hand and squeezed it.

"Lara, Jonah, Mickey, JC," Helga said slowly.

"If I have called your names, congratulations. You are the final four, and one of you will be our champion."

The Final Four

Mickey couldn't contain her excitement. She reached over and gave JC a huge bear hug, but he didn't move a muscle to hug her back. He was frozen like a statue, utterly speechless.

"JC, didn't you hear? You made it to the finals." She wasn't quite sure he was breathing!

"I think he's in shock," Lara said. "Yoo-hoo, wake up!" She gently tapped him on the shoulder.

"Here, let me try," Jonah said. He slapped JC across the cheek with his hand.

"Ouch!" JC yelped.

"There ya go—problem fixed," Jonah said. "Dude, you might actually win this thing. We all might."

"I'll need you four up here on the runway… now," Helga instructed them.

They stood before the judging panel, nervously awaiting their critique.

"Go, Mickey!" shouted a voice from the audience. She knew it was Aunt Olive.

"Your fan club?" Jonah whispered.

"Kinda. My aunt."

Helga handed her microphone to Jack, who began addressing the finalists.

"So we have four looks here from four very talented student designers. Who will win?"

"Who?" JC shouted. "Who is it?" The suspense was killing him!

"I don't know." Jack chuckled. "That's what we're trying to figure out. Why don't each of you tell us *why* you want to win *Assignment: Fashion Jr.*"

JC furrowed his brow. "What? That's not something you usually ask your contestants. Don't you want to know how and why we created our looks? I have a whole speech written…"

"Well, we're mixing things up a little," Lena explained. "We want to make sure the person we choose has a real future in fashion. Why don't you start, JC?"

JC took a deep breath. "I love fashion. I love this show. I love you guys!"

Mickey thought he was actually going to jump down off the runway and hug the judges.

"Wow, that was sweet." Helga giggled. "Thank you for that."

"Lara, you're next," Jack said.

Lara shuffled her feet nervously. "I-I…" she began. "I want to come to this country to study fashion and learn from the greatest designers in the world. I want to make a name for myself and make my family proud."

Lena nodded. "That's a lovely sentiment."

Jack looked at his list of names. "Mickey, you're up."

Mickey gulped. "Well, I've always seen fashion as a way to express myself. A lot of people have made sacrifices to get me where I am today, and I'm really grateful. I want to be a designer, not just for me, but for all of them." She looked out at the audience and saw Olive dabbing her eyes with a handkerchief.

Finally, it was Jonah's turn to speak. "I want to prove to my parents, to everyone, that fashion is my passion," he said. "I know I can be not just good but great, and I have to follow my heart. I don't want to be a lawyer. I want to be the next Karl Lagerfeld." He glanced at Mickey and smiled. "All I need is someone to believe in me."

Helga actually looked like she was getting weepy. "That was so inspiring," she said. "Okay, we have some decisions to make."

As the cameras continued rolling, the judges huddled in a corner.

"So what do you think?" Jonah asked JC. "Who's it gonna be? What does your list say?"

"I have no idea," JC replied. "Really, truly. This is unprecedented."

It took nearly twenty minutes, but finally Helga stepped onto the runway and waved a sheet of paper in her hand.

"I have here the winners of *Assignment: Fashion Jr.*," she said.

JC swooned. "This is it. This is it."

"The third runner-up is Lara," Helga announced. She handed Lara a certificate and a check, and kissed her on both cheeks. "We hope you will stay here for the summer and study. Lena wants to offer you an internship at *Teen Style* magazine in the fashion department."

Lara was over the moon. "Really? Yes, please!"

"Second runner-up goes to Mickey," Helga proclaimed. JC patted her on the back and gave her a push forward.

"Jack Rosen is very interested in having you spend a week working with him on designs for his new spring collection," Helga said.

"You have quite an eye," he told her. "And I'd love some fresh ideas."

"That would be wonderful!" Mickey said. She couldn't have asked for a better prize. She saw that JC was still standing there, eyes closed and silently praying.

"Our first runner-up, I'm delighted to say, is JC," Helga continued.

"Oh," JC said sadly. He couldn't hide his horrible disappointment. Mickey's heart broke for him.

"I might be able to cheer you up," Helga said. "I have a red carpet event in two weeks, and I was hoping you would design my outfit for it—since you know me so well."

JC's eyes lit up. "Me? You want me to design a look for you?"

Helga smiled. "If that's okay with you?"

"Okay?" JC exclaimed. "It's a dream come true!"

Jonah suddenly realized he was the last man standing.

"Which brings us to you." Helga turned to face him. "Congratulations, Jonah. You are the first champion of *Assignment: Fashion Jr.!*"

Jonah shook his head in disbelief. "Are you sure? I've never won anything in my life."

"Oh, we're sure," Jack said. "Your design was flawless—and you have an incredibly bright future ahead of you in fashion."

His parents ran up from the audience to hug him.

"That's my boy!" his dad said, throwing his arms around him. "I knew you could do it!"

"You're not disappointed that I don't want to be a lawyer?" Jonah asked.

"Disappointed?" Mrs. Zimm replied. "We couldn't be prouder. You won the whole thing!"

Aunt Olive made her way to the stage as well. "I didn't win," Mickey told her.

"So what? You win some, you lose some," Olive replied. "You impressed everyone with your talent, and that's what counts. I bet that Jack Rosen fella will offer you a job one day."

"I don't doubt it," Mr. Kaye said, coming to

congratulate his two students. "You both did exceptional work. I'm bursting with pride."

Mickey found Jonah in the crowd. "Great job!" She planted a kiss on his cheek.

"You too. So maybe I'll see you next year at FAB. My dad said they might actually let me go there."

"Oh," Mickey said softly. "I'm not sure I'll be there anymore. It's complicated."

"Huh? Jack Rosen thinks you're awesome. We all think you're awesome. Why would you quit?"

"It's my aunt." Mickey pointed to Olive who was chatting up Mr. Kaye. "She got this great job offer in LA with a big raise, and I can't let her turn it down. But I also can't live in New York by myself."

Mr. Zimm followed Mickey's finger and suddenly spied someone he recognized in the crowd. "Olive?" he asked.

"Mr. Zimm!" she replied, slightly stunned that her boss was at her niece's fashion show. "What are you doing here?"

"I could ask you the same thing," he said.

"She's my aunt," Mickey piped up. "Wait, how do you know Jonah's dad?"

"He's my boss," Olive answered.

"The boss that's making your aunt move to

LA so you can't stay at FAB and study fashion?" Jonah cried. "Dad, you can't do that!"

Mr. Zimm scratched his head. "Could everyone please calm down and tell me what you're talking about?"

"If I accept the executive position, my niece can't live with me here in New York," Olive said. "So I have to turn it down."

"What? Nonsense!" Mr. Zimm insisted. "There's no one else who can do the job, as far as I'm concerned. If you can't work out of the LA office, then I suppose you'll just have to stay here in New York."

"In a private office? With a view?" Mickey pressed him.

Jonah chuckled. "Yeah, and don't forget the big raise part."

"Yes, yes," Mr. Zimm said, shaking hands with Olive. "All the above. As long as Mickey promises to give my son a personal tour of the Fashion Academy of Brooklyn. I hear it's a remarkable place."

Mickey nodded. "It's the only place in the whole world I wanna be."

Acknowledgments

Thank you to EVERYONE who has helped us bring Fashion Academy to life—from the very first book three years ago, to this, our fifth and last one, with even an off-Broadway musical in between! It's been a lot of fun, and we hope we've inspired many young future designers to pursue their passion for fashion! We're excited for the next chapter in our mother-daughter writing career—stay tuned! Keep reading, writing, and dreaming big! XO, Sheryl and Carrie

Don't miss the rest of Mickey's fabulous fashion adventures!

About the Authors

Sheryl Berk has written about fashion for more than twenty years, first as a contributor to *InStyle* magazine and later as the founding editor in chief of *Life & Style Weekly*. She has written dozens of books with celebrities, including Britney Spears, Maddie Ziegler, and Zendaya—and the #1 *New York Times*

bestseller (turned movie) *Soul Surfer* with Bethany Hamilton. Her daughter, Carrie Berk, is a renowned cupcake connoisseur and blogger (facebook.com/PLCCupcakeClub; carriescupcake critique.shutterfly.com) with more than 100,000 followers at the age of thirteen! Carrie is a fountain of fabulous ideas for book series—she came up with Fashion Academy in the fifth grade. Carrie learned to sew from her grandma "Gaga" and has outfitted many an American Girl doll in original fashions. The Berks also write the deliciously popular series The Cupcake Club.